Basics of Business Management series

Booklet 1

Introduction to Business and Management

(Laying the foundations)

A.S. Srinivasan

Clever Fox
PUBLISHING

Chennai • Bangalore

CLEVER FOX PUBLISHING
Chennai, India

Published by CLEVER FOX PUBLISHING 2023
Copyright © A.S.Srinivasan 2023

Introduction to Business and Management

Based on my booklet **A Concise Guide to Basics of Business Management,** I thought it would be appropriate to outline major concepts and practices under each functional area as well as business strategy in greater detail in the form of booklets. Thus, along with the Concise Guide, these booklets will give a more detailed coverage of these concepts in the field of business management.

Of course, each concept in itself has been covered and discussed in great detail by many scholars and there are innumerable books on each of them. No one small booklet like this one, can claim to do justice to all of them in a few pages. This is just a distilled and brief outline of them which again is intended to give an overview of these classic concepts so that the reader becomes familiar with them.

I have reproduced my Introduction, References and Afterword from my booklet **A Concise Guide to Basics of Business Management** since these booklets will also serve the same purpose to the same audience and are from the same sources. Nothing stated here are original and are based entirely on the materials mentioned in Introduction. I was fortunate to have had the opportunity to study them. Where necessary, I have taken the liberty of using them to preserve their meaning. The errors and misunderstandings are purely results of my limited knowledge and exposure.

Booklet One in this series is on **Introduction to Business and Management** which briefly introduces topics like what we mean by business and management, business model and aspects of managing and creating value. These will be further covered in subsequent booklets. This booklet sets the stage for your onward journey in your quest for understanding the field of management.

A.S. Srinivasan   **October, 2022**

A Concise Guide to Basics of Business Management

Introduction

This booklet will be of use to all those who are interested in the field of Business Management. If you are a practising manager or an entrepreneur, this could serve as a refresher. If you have recently taken up a managerial position, this will be a useful reference book for you to look at some of the concepts mentioned here. If you are a student or a person interested to know the basics of management, this will serve the purpose of a guidebook.

This booklet is brief but comprehensive, outlining all the major management concepts and practices in all functional areas. As a manager in today's highly competitive and dynamic business environment, you need to

1. *Develop the capability to look at your organisation's business holistically*

2. *Become familiar with major concepts and practices in all functional areas of management*

3. *Understand the integrated nature of your business, the interconnectedness of various functions and the impact of your individual and departmental decisions and actions on the total operations of the company and*

4. *Have the urge to develop yourself further to meet the challenges of today and tomorrow*

Hopefully, this booklet will help you embark on this journey of life-long learning.

I have primarily relied on various management books by leading authors in compiling all the concepts presented here which I gratefully acknowledge. I claim no originality or ownership of these ideas. I have gathered these over the years I was serving in academics. I have appended a list of primary references and have mentioned the names of original thinkers and writers in my text at appropriate places. There are many more that are in public domain which I have used in presenting these contents.

All these classic concepts have been mentioned very briefly and need further study for greater understanding. This is in no way a textbook. It is just a window to the field of management. This booklet will have served its purpose if it arouses your curiosity to know more on any topic or concept you are interested in. I look forward to receiving your comments and feedback.

Welcome to a short journey through this fascinating field of management!

A.S. Srinivasan **October, 2022**

Introduction to Business and Management

In this booklet, we aim to introduce and define the meaning and scope of what we mean by business and management. As we will be seeing shortly, when people get together to perform various activities required to carry on a business, a business entity or organisation is formed and it becomes the basic unit of business. Managing the activities of the business unit is the job of management. Booklets that follow deal with various aspects of this in detail. Here, we will consider the following broad questions while outlining the concepts and practices of business and management:

1.   What is business?

2.   What is your business model?

3.   What is managing?

4.   What is performance?

5.   What are the components of creating value and making money?

1.   What is business?

1.1   A way of looking at business:

We can define business as an activity carried out by an individual or a group of people aimed at fulfilling a perceived customer need or want for the purpose of

i.   Making profits year-on-year and

ii.   Adding on to the wealth of promoters who invest money (financial resources) in the business

To carry out various activities of business, people get together forming a business entity. We will be using the words firm, company, enterprise, business and organisation interchangeably to denote a business entity.

1.2   Basic determinants of success of a business entity:

Profits and wealth creation depend on what the firm or company or organisation offers to its customers towards fulfilling their needs or wants. The questions that need to be answered here are:

i.   Does the perceived customer need really exist?

ii.   Does the company's offering (products and services) fulfil the need better than competition?

iii.   Does the company have a competitive advantage over its competitors on a sustainable basis to continue to earn profits and create wealth over the long term?

iv.   These also depend on the nature of company's business, its work inputs, resources and capabilities. This means that what resources the organisation has and how capable it is of putting them together to deliver a higher value to its customers.

v.   They also depend on risks involved in operating the business and what Returns can be expected commensurate with risks taken.

2.   What is the nature of your business?

2.1   Classification of business organisations:

The term business can mean different things. It could denote an individual company, an industry, a particular industry sector or the entire business world.

i.   Based on the sector, normally an organisation can be classified under:

- Private sector
- Public sector
- Co-operative sector
- Not-for-profit sector

This is based on ownership pattern and purpose. It is worthwhile noting here that even not-for-profit businesses have to make surpluses on a sustainable basis to meet current costs and make investments for the future without depending solely on donations and charities.

ii.   Businesses are classified based on the nature of their offering such as:

- Manufacturing organisation
- Services organisation
- Product or service organisation depending on the nature of primary offering

In most of the cases, there are no pure product or service organisations since there is a mix of both in their offerings.

iii. Firms are also classified on the basis of their ownership such as:

- Proprietorship, firm owned by one individual
- Partnership, firm owned by a group of individuals with unlimited liability
- Private Limited company, again by a group of individuals in limited numbers with limited liability
- Public Limited company where ownership is spread through a large number of investors called shareholders

iv.   When a company is formed, it becomes a separate entity.

- Its owners or promoters bring in capital which is called equity. What they borrow from outsiders or financial institutions is called debt. Thus, the capital employed is the total of equity plus debt.

- Being a separate entity, the company is governed by commercial laws.

- When a firm is small, its operations are looked after directly by the owners/promoters. As the firm grows bigger, they are run by employed managers.

2.2   Laws governing business organisations:

Some of the important laws governing a business are:

- Company/corporate laws

- Contract laws

- Sale of Goods laws

- Consumer protection laws

- Tax laws

- Constitutional laws

2.3   Agency theory:

When a company is run by managers as in the case of most large organisations, there is often conflict between the interests of owners/shareholders and managers their "Agents". Possible areas of conflict are:

- Time horizon: While shareholders' needs include long term growth, managers often tend to take a short-term view for immediate profits and thereby immediate rewards. Hence the term short-termism is used to describe the attitude of managers who concentrate on quarter-to-quarter results.

- Rewards and perquisites: Often managers demand much higher levels than what is in the best interests of owners.

- Attitude to risk: A risk-averse company may end up managed by high risk-taking managers which may put the entire equity at risk.

- Information asymmetry: Since managers are in control of day-to-day operations, they have current information on developments rather than owners/shareholders who are away from business and get the information later. This leads to manipulation by managers which may not be in the best interests of the owners.

All these lead to what is called "moral hazard" and are covered under Agency Theory. However, external environment and business laws should provide necessary checks and balances.

2.4 Organising a business:

Managing various activities of a business organisation is often organised along business functions such as:

- Manufacturing and Operations Management

- Sales and Marketing Management

- Financial Management

- Human Resources Management

Other ways of organising business depend on the nature of business and primary activities.

Generally, Management schools teach basics of Management along functional lines with other basic sciences like Mathematics, Statistics, Accounting, Psychology and Economics in the first year. Later on, they go on to advanced topics on these functional areas and other integrative subjects like

Business Strategy during the second year. You can see that my approach is based on similar lines of functional approach for covering various topics in management.

While companies are organised along these functional lines to ensure that each function gets expert and in-depth attention, they are further integrated by cross-functional teams and general managers to achieve overall objectives of the company. But in reality, people start working in so-called "silos" thinking of their functional goals only and not considering their impact on the organisation as a whole. This leads to inter-functional conflicts resulting in sub-optimal results overall. We will be seeing more of this on the next booklet on Business Organisations.

3. Multiple stakeholders and multiple expectations:

3.1 Profit as the primary purpose:

i.   We started by saying that the primary purpose of business is to make profits and add on to the wealth of owners or promoters. In line with this, many management experts have maintained that "business of business is business only". This has been the dominant view of for-profit, private organisations and their operations are geared towards achieving this over-arching purpose. In other words, they say that organisations work primarily to fulfil the expectations of shareholders only.

ii. However, we know that apart from shareholders, there are several other groups of people who are also interested in the operations and continued existence of the organisation. But their primary expectations are different from that of shareholders of making profits only.

iii. All these persons interested in robust operations and existence of the company are called stakeholders. Primary stakeholder groups and their expectations are:

Stakeholders	Primary expectations
• Owners or shareholders	Financial return
• Employees	Pay
• Customers	Value for money
• Creditors who lend money	Credit worthiness and prompt repayment
• Suppliers who supply raw material etc.	On-time payments and regular orders
• Government	Job creation, Compliance with laws
• Community	Jobs, safety

3.2 Dominant stakeholder interests:

At different times, interests of different stakeholders dominated the business scene based on prevailing conditions. For example, in the first half of the 20th century, it was workers' group that dominated. Later on, towards the end of the century, the focus was on customer interests. Of late, it is environmental concern shared by everyone, that is dominating the scene. But all along right from the beginning, most of the companies are dominated by the view that their primary purpose is to make profits and enhance shareholder value even at the cost some other stakeholders' interests.

If we pass for a minute to reflect, we may see that this can be achieved only when interests of all stakeholders are met at least to the threshold levels. However, companies still work on unstated premise that only by ensuring profits, they will be able to meet expectations of all stakeholders. The right approach may be to work for optimisation of profits and not maximisation of profits at the cost of any other stakeholder group. A balanced approach is called for.

4.   What is performance?

Given this scenario of multiple stakeholders and multiple expectations- some of them quantifiable and some of them not, we have to decide how we can define and measure performance of the company that can achieve this balance.

4.1   The basic approach:

A basic principle in management is that in order to control anything, you need to measure it. As we know, the most easily measurable and tangible measure is financial performance since all other stakeholders' interests have a measure of subjectivity. Hence historically emphasis has always been on financial performance only.

But with greater pressure from all stakeholder groups, new approaches, frameworks and measures to performance measurement have been developed like the Balanced Scorecard, the European Foundation for Quality Management (EFQM) excellence model, Triple bottom line, Environmental, Social and Governance (ESG) indices etc. While some companies have adopted them, it is still financial measures that are used to judge the performance of a company as reflected by its share price in the stock market. We cover this in greater detail in Managing Finance booklet that will follow.

4.2   A broader approach to measuring performance:

A more general approach that indicates whether the company is heading in the right direction is described below.

i.   Effectiveness: Is the organisation moving in the right direction? Is it doing the right things?

ii.   Efficiency: Is it doing it right? It is a measure of input of resources and results achieved as a ratio.

iii.   Economy: Is it able to perform economically? Does it manage its costs of inputs?

iv.   Ethics: Do the actions of the organisation and its members conform to accepted social norms of morality?

v.   Equity: Does it treat all its employees equitably without any favour or prejudice?

4.3   Developing holistic approach:

Our discussions on performance measurement so far, would indicate that we need to develop a holistic view of business which considers the expectations of all its stakeholders. We look at two concepts or frameworks that help in developing this holistic approach to business.

- Systems thinking. A further development on this is called Design thinking

- Contingency theory

4.4   The concept of systems thinking:

This calls for following practices:

i.   Holistic approach: This is based on the principle of synergy which means to say that the whole is greater than sum of its individual parts. This is especially true in the case of organisations since they are based on differentiating various tasks and then integrating them for optimal performance. It requires one to look at all aspects of the issue, take a broader view of business before plunging into the details straight away with a narrow focus.

Sadly, this capability to develop systems thinking is often missing in companies and their executives. As we saw earlier, managers are used to working in "silos" and do not see beyond their function to study and understand the impact of their decisions on performance of organisation as a whole.

ii. Following this we can say that systems thinking involves inter-disciplinary thinking. In most of complex business situations, simple linear cause and effect analysis does not suffice. Several apparently unrelated causes may lead to multiple effects and a simple solution aimed at solving an issue, may adversely affect performance of the organisation elsewhere. For example, while the marketing person may reduce price to achieve his/her sales targets, it will affect the overall profits of the company and also production may not have the capacity to produce required extra quantities apart from causing bottlenecks in procurement, manpower and customer service. One needs to develop capability to think laterally and not just linearly.

iii. Systems thinking also involves looking at the problem from different perspectives which may lead to the conclusion that real issue lies elsewhere. This is achieved by reframing the issues and considering at all aspects to arrive at the root cause.

iv. Finally, systems thinking will be enhanced by developing and also re-examining our own mental maps and models to look at multiple cause-effect situations and solutions.

4.5 Contingency theory:

The other general approach that will be of help in finding solutions to complex issues is called contingency theory which states that there is no one best way to solve problems. Contrasting this, people may take one of the following extreme views:

i. There is one best way to solve a problem which is called the universal view. People take the same approach for different problems under the belief that it is the best approach.

ii. The other is the case view which implies that every situation is unique and calls for unique solution.

Between these lies the contingency view which states that there are logical patterns in business situations, and we can develop similar responses to similar problems.

4.6 Organisational contingencies:

Building on this premise, we can say that there is no one best way of running a business and "one size fits all", quick-fix solutions will not help all organisations and even those within the same industry. We have to look at the following factors which may be different for different organisations:

i. Task, technology and scale: What business is the company in? What technology does it use? At what scale does it operate? Solutions for problems in a small-scale industry with minimal technological inputs, more human power oriented and producing components may be quite different from those for a large, highly technology-oriented, producing a fully integrated product line organisation.

ii. Environment: What is the environment in which the company operates? Here it is worthwhile thinking whether we can succeed in our country just by bringing in and copying western practices in toto.

iii. Goals and strategy: Even within an industry, one may go in for low-cost, high-volume strategy while another may go in for high-value, low-volume strategy. Obviously, solutions for problems in these companies will be different.

iv. Culture and structure: Solutions for problems in a highly centralised, hierarchical organisation will be different from those in a decentralised, flat organisation.

And to add to further complexity, these factors are inter-related.

4.7. Framework for organisational analysis:

The much-celebrated management consulting company McKinsey had developed a fairly robust framework for analysing organisations called McKinsey's 7 S framework which has stood the test of time. The 7 S factors are:

i. Strategy

ii. Structure

iii. Systems

iv. Styles

v. Staff

vi. Skills

and most importantly,

vii. Shared values which would include its vision, mission, goals and objectives shared by all members.

5. What is your business model?

A business model outlines how an organisation creates value. While we will discuss more on value in a while, as we saw earlier, the firm has to create value first, deliver part of value created to its customers and capture the balance for its shareholders as profit, balancing the expectations of all stakeholders.

We can define business model based on answers to the following questions:

i.   What is the firm offering? (Offering in terms of products and services)

ii. To whom does the company offer its products and services? (Target customers)

iii. How does it create value, deliver it to customers and capture surplus value? (Infrastructure, finance, costs and profits)

We will now see each of them in some detail.

6. What is the company offering to its customers?

6.1 Value equation:

As we saw, an organisation can fulfil its purpose of making profits and creating wealth to the owners only by fulfilling a customer need or want and retaining them by offering customers a value higher than what competition or others offer. This is the basic premise on which all businesses operate to remain viable. We can further define customer value through an equation as

Customer value = Benefits - Costs

6.2 Benefits offered to customers consist of the following:

i.   The product or service offered that meets with their requirements in terms of price, performance, functions, features, technical innovation, product/service assurance through creating and managing brands etc.

ii. Availability and reliability of supplies on time and in quantities required.

iii. And overall experience with the product and company in terms of services, solutions and other intangible factors like brand associations etc.

iv. The costs incurred by the customer include price paid, other acquisition costs like transport, maintenance etc, payment terms in terms of credit facilities, discounts offered and ease of getting the product.

v. Organisations can prosper only when they are able to create or discover value, deliver part of value to customers and retain balance as can see be seen below:

Value discovery consists of developing a product or service that provides a value which is greater than that offered by the next best competitor in that class.

Value delivered which is also called as consumer surplus, is the additional value offered to the customers over the nearest alternative, from the value discovered as above.

Value retained or captured which is also called as producer surplus, is the balance of value discovered less value delivered to the target customer. We can express this by the following equations:

Customer value = Product + Access + experience

Value retained or captured = Value discovered or created – Value delivered to customers

6.3 Concept of value proposition:

i. Another basic business premise is that you cannot be everything to everybody. This means to say that a company has to develop its business strategy based on what kind of customers it chooses to service and what value it would offer to these customers that will satisfy their expectations. While these will be covered in detail in the booklet on Marketing Management, here we will look at this general concept developed by management authors Treacy and Wiersema in 1996.

ii. The value proposition is an implicit promise the company makes to its customers to deliver a particular combination of values - price, quality performance, selection, convenience, service etc. By knowing the preferences of its customers, the company develops its strategy to offer a value or a set of values that will offer them greater satisfaction.

iii. The authors further go on to define three dominant value disciplines or value propositions offered by market leaders to dominate the market. They are Product leadership, Operational excellence and Customer intimacy.

iv. Companies that follow the strategy of product leadership offer their customers the very best product or service in their category in terms of functions/features, performance, technical innovation etc. and they continue to do this year after year.

v. Companies that offer operational excellence provide reasonable products at their best price and least inconvenience to customers. Their promise is low price and trouble-free service.

vi. Companies who opt for customer intimacy, concentrate on specific customers and not the whole market, cultivate relationships and meet their unique needs. They offer these customers the best solution.

While they may overlap, these are the three dominant value propositions offered by market leaders.

6.4   Business strategy:

i.   Arising out of above approaches, companies decide on their basic business strategy. Basically, according to Prof. Michael Porter, one of the most celebrated strategy gurus, companies follow one of the two basic strategies called generic strategies. They could choose either cost leadership or differentiation. Under cost leadership, companies practise operational efficiency and are able to offer to their customers comparable quality as their nearest competitor at a lower price or at the lowest cost. Thus, they become cost leaders. Alternatively, companies can choose differentiation strategy by which they offer the best products in their category in terms of differentiating them from competition at acceptable prices to the customers and become leaders in their category and industry.

ii.   Further, with advent of more sophisticated marketing research tools and techniques, companies are able to gain greater consumer insight or market insight. This enables them to understand the preferences of their target customers better and develop an altogether new product concept and positioning in an over-crowded market. This strategy developed by Professors W Chan Kim and Renee Mauborgne is called the blue ocean strategy and helps companies take leadership position in hitherto unchartered territory aptly described as Blue Ocean.

We will see more on these in the following booklet on Organisations.

7. **The customer:**
   (to whom does the company offer its products and services?)

Marketing persons assert that the most important person in the organisation is the customer since the organisation exists primarily to satisfy his/her needs. Without customers, the company will cease to exist. It is true that a company can hope to make profits and grow only if it continues to deliver value and satisfaction to its customers.

While some companies deliver their offering directly to customers, in many instances they reach them through intermediary channels. These are called distribution channels which are involved in delivering the product or service from the manufacturer to the customer.

In understanding and satisfying our customers, we need to answer the following questions:

i.   Who are our target customers?

ii.   What are their needs and wants that we are trying to satisfy?

iii. How do we ensure that our offering reaches the customer- what channels do we employ?

iv.   How do we maintain our relationships with our customers and service their requirements for their complete satisfaction and manage our brands which connect us to the customers?

v.   How do we meet competition so that we continue to offer a higher value to our customers than competitors?

vi.   How do we forecast demand and how do we develop our marketing strategies and plans?

In the present highly competitive and dynamic business environment, firming up our answers to these questions and revisiting them periodically are vital for continued successful existence of the company. These are discussed in detail in the booklet on Marketing Management in this series.

8.   Company's infrastructure:
(How do we discover (create), deliver and capture (retain) value?)

8.1   Resources of an organisation:

An organisation delivers value to all its stakeholders using certain resources at its disposal and putting them all together to create and deliver value. The main resources a company can bring in are:

i.   Financial: cash resources, accessibility to financial markets like banks and other financial institutions, private lenders (sources of debt) and stock markets (equity) etc

ii.   Physical: it invests part of these financial resources into plant & equipment, technology, R & D etc

iii.   Legal: It can hold patents, copyrights, licences, trademarks etc

iv.   Human: People resources combine all the other resources to deliver value. They consist of number of employees, their knowledge, skills, commitment etc

v.   Organisation: This includes the structural strengths, cultural characteristics, managerial and leadership competences etc

vi.   Relational: An organisation's relationships and networks with its customers, shareholders, employees, creditors, suppliers etc serve as a major resource.

vii.   Informational: In modern data driven business world, knowledge about business environment, customer preferences and emerging trends, competition etc is a great resource.

Resources by themselves do not produce results. But a combination of resources brought together in an optimal mix for the tasks on hand, produces the results expected. This is called capability. Thus, while resources form the basis of firm's capabilities, capabilities alone give it competitive advantage. This means that by building up its capabilities, the company is able to do better than competition in delivering value to its customers and thereby achieve desired results.

8.2   Value chain:

Value chain is a concept used for analysing your own organisation by breaking it down into sequential parts like procurement, technology, human resources, finance, marketing etc and ascertain value added by each part or link in the chain. This will help in identifying where your organisation is doing better or worse than competition and improve it better to deliver greater value. In other words, value chain analysis leads to developing competitive advantage.

Companies also have their own partnerships to deliver customer value, like suppliers, distribution channels etc. Thus, we say that when companies compete with one another, their entire value chains compete because value discovery can take place anywhere along the supply chain including partners.

All these components go into a company's infrastructure which reveals how it combines its resources along with partners to gain competitive advantage and deliver superior value. The whole concept of business strategy is based on this gaining competitive advantage since business is all about competition. This will be discussed in greater detail in booklet on Organisations.

9.   Finance:
(cost structure, revenues and profits and time value)

They say that ultimately a company is judged by its bottom-line meaning profits. But profits arise out of investments made, costs incurred, selling prices and revenue streams and importantly, when each of these takes place. Following questions need to be addressed in evaluating company's financial component of its business model.

i.   What are our investments and returns? Sources of finance, sales realisations and profits

ii.   What is our cost structure? In terms of raw materials, labour, overheads etc.

iii.   What are our revenue streams? Selling prices and margins, money realised through our sales and services and when we realise them (cash flows)

Since all parameters are measured under one common measure viz. money, booklet on Financial Management will cover all these questions.

10.   What is Managing?
(What do you do as a manager?)

We now move on to the next topic of this booklet on Managing. We can broadly say that essence of management is managing people and managing resources to achieve desired results. As we know, people are different from other resources and hence managing people or human relations is by itself the primary responsibility of management that should facilitate managing other resources.

Managing people is a social activity. Integrating and improving performance of other people to make things happen towards achievement of goals as per plans is the primary job of every manager. Thus, in a classic sense, managing was more of a co-ordinating and general activity.

However, the modern management scene is far different and much more complicated than this simple approach. With changing technologies over decades and much more rapidly in the present times, especially in Communication and Information technologies and emerging new digital world, the nature of management has changed to include specialists as well as general managers. Other major factors that are changing the way we manage are:

i.   Dynamic global economic conditions

ii.   Growing and at the same time contracting globalisation and liberalisation of trade across all countries and their interconnectedness

iii.   Changing demographics in terms of consumer profiles, their preferences and expectations

iv.   Greater demand from all stakeholders leading to more legislations and societal pressures for conformance and performance

These have naturally impacted the job of a manager and old ways of doing things may not hold good any longer. There is a need for managers to re-invent themselves and update their knowledge continuously.

Notwithstanding this need, we will look at the managerial job under three broad dimensions:

i.   The content

ii.   The process

iii.   The context

10.1 The content:

Here we look at the managerial job in terms of the roles played by the manager since they carry out their activities as per demands of their roles or what is expected of them. A much-celebrated management thinker Prof. Henry Mintzberg had defined three major roles played by the manager:

- Interpersonal roles defining their relationships with others

- Informational roles whereby the manager collects, interprets and transmits information

- Decisional roles: Here Managers are expected to make decisions regarding use of resources under their control and implement them.

Under each of these, he had developed sub-roles as under:

i.   Interpersonal roles:

  - Figurehead: Here the manager holds the formal position and authority that goes with it and represents her/his group, team, function or company.

  - Leader: The manager brings together the needs/goals of the organisation and of people reporting to her/him to ensure achievement of goals through teamwork.

  - Liaison: Here the manager is expected to maintain relationships with her/his peers, bosses and people outside the organisation.

ii.   Informational roles:

- Monitor: Here the manager follows up on what goes on within the organisation as well as in the external environment.

- Disseminator: Following monitoring, the manager interprets and passes on the information gathered to her/his team members.

- Spokesperson: Under this role, the manager gives information about the organisation to outsiders.

iii.   Decisional roles: Managers are expected to play following roles in ensuring successful operations of the company:

- Entrepreneur: In this role, the manager takes decisions on what is happening in the company, decides what needs to be done and initiates changes.

- Disturbance handler: Meeting the challenges that are beyond control, planning response and handling such situations form part of this role.

- Resource allocator: Allocating resources of the organisation to the tasks on hand in terms of money, manpower and scheduling activities come under this role.

- Negotiator: In this role, the manager is expected to decide on where, when and how much to commit organisational resources to the demands made.

As we can see, with ever-changing business environment, the importance of different roles changes with time. Also, all managers need not play all roles in all jobs in all organisations and the roles they play predominantly depend on the organisation and their own job. However, this framework can be used to look at one's own work and see areas where one can perform her/his role better.

10.2 The Process of Managing:

In his classical definition, Mr. Henry Fayol, one of the pioneers of management thinking in the early days, gave his definition of managing which is called the rational view of management as given below:

i.   To manage is:

- to forecast and plan: examining future and planning course of action

- to organise: procuring necessary material and manpower resources

- to command: ensuring activity among people as per plan

- to co-ordinate: bringing all activities together to achieve results

- to control: making sure everything is done as per established rules and command

ii.   "Scientific management": A further extension of this called the scientific management as espoused by Mr. Fredrick Taylor, states that "there is one best way of doing any job. Improvement of efficiency is the main concern of management."

We must look at these in the context of time when maximising output with given inputs was the primary task of management. Those were the days of sellers' markets controlled and serviced by financial entrepreneurs and/or engineers.

We now know that this "command and control" model will not work in modern times though you may be surprised to see that these are the underlying assumptions on which many managers operate.

10.3 The context of managing:

Here we use a framework developed by Ms. Rosemary Stewart, another management writer. Her framework states that what work a manager does, how and when she/he does it and what new initiatives the manager undertakes or what choices she/he has are in the context of demands and constraints made.

i.   Demands: As a manager, demands made on you may be:

- Externally imposed
- System imposed
- Your manager/boss imposed
- Peer imposed
- Staff people reporting to you imposed
- Your own self-imposed

ii.   Constraints: You may have to work under following constraints:

- Legal and contractual regulations
- Resource limitations
- Organisational policies and procedures
- Technological limitations
- Locational limitations

Now in two jobs- both with same constraints but with different demands, you will have greater choices where the demands are relatively lower. Conversely, where demands remain the same, but constraints vary, your freedom is more where constraints are relatively lower. This is true in the case of similar jobs in different organisations as well.

Thus, the context in which you operate dictates your choices of what you do.

11. The reality:

11.1 Successful vs. Effective managers:

Yet another input on managing, highlighting the differences between successful and effective managers, was given by Prof. Fred Luthans. According to him, the "real" managers are primarily engaged in:

- Traditional management activities viz. decision making, planning and controlling

- Communication activities consisting of exchanging routine information and related documentation

- Human resources management activities of staffing, training, disciplining, motivating and managing conflicts

- Networking with people inside and outside the organisation

His theory is that the so-called successful managers (based on promotions within the company) spent most of the time in networking and the least, in human resources management. He goes on to say that "effective managers" defined in terms of their qualitative and quantitative job performance and the satisfaction and commitment of people working under them, spent most of their time in communication and human resources management activities and the least in networking. As they say, in many companies in the case of promotions, whom you know seems to be more important than what you actually know and do.

11.2 What managers really do:

To cap at all these "confusing" ways of looking at managerial job, Prof. Henry Mintzberg says that in reality, managers jump from one activity to another, working in fragmented short intervals, often interrupted even then. A manager can never say that his job is finished. Prof. Mintzberg compares the job of a manager to that of conductor of an orchestra.

This takes us to the reality of management which can be described as below:

i.   it is complex: The complexity arises out of Nature of problems, Problem solving process and Accountability.

Nature of problems and Problem-solving process: Problems can be simple (or bounded) where the difficulties are smaller and well-defined. Its implications are limited. Here the problem-solving process is straight and simple with linear relationship.

On the other hand, complex (or messy) problems have multiple causes and solution for one cause will have effect on another. This is called multiple and mutual causation and effect to mean that each is not restricted to a particular situation but has wide implications. In such cases, defining the problem, analysing the causes and arriving at solutions are complex.

Hence, for complex problems instead of spending all their time to find the best solution, managers just implement a satisfactory solution. This is called satisficing and it may not lead to the most rational solution, but a workable one.

ii.   Accountability: As we saw earlier, managers are responsible for meeting the demands of all stakeholders at least to their minimum acceptable levels or "threshold tolerance" levels for each, thus balancing their interests to arrive at acceptable and satisfactory solutions. This is yet another source of complexity.

iii.   It is highly human behaviour oriented: The manager has to work through groups and manage conflicts within the group in the context of organisational politics which is inevitable. He/she has to be a part of the group but at the same time stand apart to have an objective view of the situation. This can even be more complex and stressful in the case of a newly promoted manager who has to work with and lead other group members who were his/her peers earlier.

These are the factors that make managing a complex exercise.

We will now move on to some of the approaches, practices, tools and techniques that help in the job of a manager.

12.   A structured approach to managing:

If the essence of management is to make things happen, the first steps a manager needs to take are given in the following 4 stage process:

- Set objectives and targets
- Plan, identify tasks to be done and implement linking people and resources
- Monitor on a continuing basis the progress towards achievement of targets and objectives
- Take necessary action based on results- modifying tasks to be done, revising the targets etc.

This process is called the control loop and the steps repeated until expected results are achieved. This is similar to the much-celebrated Japanese management tool called the P-D-C-A cycle (Plan-Do-Check-Act or Plan-Do-Check-Adjust).

12.1 Setting objectives:

While setting the objectives, managers should take care to ensure that they are SMART which stands for:

S: Specific - We should specify clearly the specific results to be achieved to avoid ambiguity

M: Measurable - We should be able to measure inputs and outputs in quantifiable terms

A: Agreed - They should be agreed upon by the jobholder

R: Realistic - Targets set and agreed upon should be achievable and not out of reach

T: Time-bound - We should specify starting and end time limits since time is probably the most important resource

12.2 Planning:

It is generally said that a sound plan has a much greater chance of success. In developing such plans, managers use several tools and techniques that help them break the tasks down and execute them on a time-bound scale.

Mind maps, Tasks breakdown charts, Critical path analysis etc. are some of the tools used to improve planning. Other techniques used by managers include Potential problem analysis where likelihood of specific problems occurring and their impact are analysed and necessary plans made. Similarly, Contingency planning helps in reacting to unanticipated adverse developments. Often, managers keep two plans- Plan A which is the one to be implemented and in case of unforeseen developments, Plan B which will help in meeting the challenges posed.

12.3 Monitoring:

Continuous monitoring involves regular observation of activities that go on, questioning and discussing with the job performer on any difficulties and approaches to solving them, generating and analysing reports on periodic basis, maintenance of necessary records and analysis of findings etc. Very often, this is the missing link in organisations and corrective actions are taken too late in meeting the challenges that arise.

13.   Classical Problem-solving approach:

In a broad sense. Problem-solving and Opportunity finding are considered as primary functions of managers- problem-solving to ensure that current operations are carried out as per plan so that they deliver desired results while opportunity finding is to find new avenues for growth for the organisation.

Classical problem-solving approach as taught in business schools and as practised by business organisations consists of following steps:

i.   Identify and define the problem

ii.   Set objectives and targets to overcome the problem and generate alternatives to overcome the problem

iii.   Analyse the various alternatives available in terms of targets set and factors involved and make necessary decisions

iv.   Communicate and implement the decision and plan of action

v.   Monitor and control

14. Creative Problem Solving:

14.1 Stages:

Since today's business problems are often complex, we may need to look at other approaches for finding solutions to these problems involving complexity, hence the popularity of Creative Problem Solving (CPS) techniques. A creative problem-solving approach consists of a few steps as described below to ensure that all related and unrelated issues are considered and all possible solutions are generated. At each stage, we begin by diverging, that is, looking from all angles and then converge to arrive at the most appropriate action.

i.　　Stage 1: Problem exploration
　　　Open up (diverge): Explore different angles
　　　Close down (converge): Select key problem

ii.　　Stage 2: Ideas generation
　　　Open up (diverge): Consider all alternative ideas
　　　Close down (converge): Select preferred option

iii.　　Stage 3: Plan implementation
　　　Open up (diverge): Plan all supporting actions
　　　Close down (converge): Prioritise and implement important ones

iv.　　Stage 4: Evaluation
　　　Open up (diverge): Monitor progress in all areas
　　　Close down (converge): Modify specific actions

14.2 Techniques of CPS:

Several techniques are used at each stage of creative problem-solving process like

i. Brain-storming: to generate several ideas by opening up the mind as well in a group of people

ii. Lateral thinking: to look at things from different perspectives in unstructured and free ways

iii. Decision trees to look at impact of various decisions

iv. Cause and effect diagrams: to arrive at necessary actions on monitoring

While both classical rational problem-solving and creative problem-solving approaches follow similar steps, the latter helps in broadening one's thinking where new, novel and unbounded ways of thinking are encouraged and consequently, different, new solutions emerge in complex situations. However, we should bear in mind that both call for disciplined thinking. As we say, perspiration is 99% and inspiration is just 1%!

15. Components of creating value and making profits:

We will conclude this booklet by giving an overview of the various elements that go into creating value and making profits in a start-up or running organisation. These elements will be discussed in detail in booklets that follow covering all functional areas.

The major components that are to be considered in this exercise are:

i. Forecasting/anticipating customer need/want for a product or service and estimating/projecting demand in the short, medium and long terms. This will form the basis for planning the enterprise based on the feasibility of the venture, determining objectives for the organisation and resources required, overall business strategy to achieve these objectives and detailed functional plans

ii.   Acquiring necessary financial and other resources, making investments and starting up the enterprise in conformance with above plans, legal requirements and stakeholder mandate.

iii.   Managing operations and technology for turning out intended products and services.

iv.   Marketing these to the customers with our extended distribution channels, managing customer relations and brands

v.   Managing financial requirements, costs, cash flows, profits and growth

vi.   Managing and developing human relations which is most critical in carrying out all above functions

Let us now take a brief look at steps involved in each of the above components.

15.1 Forecasting/anticipating customer demand:

i.   Researching the market through formal and informal techniques

ii.   Deciding on the target customer segments

iii.   Developing the offering based on chosen customer segment demand forecasts and importantly on company's resources and capabilities

iv.   Keeping track of developments in external environment and competition, competitors' and our market shares etc.

v.   Developing new products/services on a continuous basis to meet emerging customer needs and technological developments

15.2 Making investments and starting up:

i. Deciding on resources required to meet anticipated demand

ii. Bringing in necessary financial investments to create required resources through own (equity) and borrowed (debt) long-term and short-term funds as and when required

iii. Understanding legal requirements

iv. Ensuring all resources are in place, commencing operations and move towards stabilising them

15.3 Managing operations and supply chain:

i. Getting the right technology, plant and machinery

ii. Finalising the specifications of the offering and planning for manufacture with necessary human resources and support services

iii. Manufacturing as per specifications to meet customer expectations in terms of quality, quantity, delivery time and cost

iv. Managing costs

v. Upgrading existing technology and offerings by bringing in new products through continuous R & D

15.4 Marketing the offering:

i. Developing and implementing appropriate competitive marketing strategy in terms of product, price, place (distribution) and promotion (including advertising)

ii. Managing sales and distribution functions

iii. Developing and maintaining customer relations on a continuing basis

iv.   Creating and managing brands that reinforce company's positioning in the minds of the customers to enjoy competitive advantage

v.   Integrating and managing all communication efforts with all stakeholders

All these are essential to ensure customer satisfaction and achievement of targets.

15.5 Managing finances of the company:

Ultimately, the main objective of the firm is to make profits and add on to the wealth of owners. Since all results are measured in money terms, managing finances becomes critical. Major aspects to be considered are:

i.   Managing costs and margins

ii.   Managing cash flows and cash reserves

iii.   Managing resources utilisation for optimum turnaround of money invested

iv.   Bringing in long-term and short-term funds as required

v.   Appraising projects for investments in terms of funds required and returns expected on a time scale

vi.   Measuring performance and reporting deviations and shortfalls and maintaining relevant data and information

vii.   Ensuring compliance with all legal requirements

15.6 Managing human resources:

People make things happen and hence managing human resources is central to all managers' jobs. This covers the following:

i.   Planning the required organisational structure and defining jobs by breaking down tasks to be carried out

ii.   Recruiting, selecting and placing appropriate persons for these jobs

iii.   Motivating, managing performance, training & development and succession plans

iv.   Building a high-performance culture to achieve results

This in a nutshell, highlights the components that go into creating value and making profits. You can see that we have broken them down along functional lines. It is obvious that they are neither linear nor can be put in neat little boxes. Most of them are inter-functional. It is the primary responsibility of top management to integrate the efforts of all functions so that company's goals are achieved.

Having seen what we mean by business in a broad sense and what is managing, we will be discussing major aspects of each functional area in the booklets that follow. Before that, we will be covering the topic of Organisations in Booklet 2, since they are basic the units of business and managing and lead to integrating the efforts of all people and functions towards achievement of objectives of business.

Afterword

I started writing the booklet on Basics of Business Management and subsequent booklets covering each block by end of 2019. So far, I have completed four booklets and two more remain. The Covid 19 pandemic hit the world right through this period of end 2019, whole of 2020, 2021 and third and fourth waves are on us right now since January 2022. It has shaken the very basics of our lives to a great extent. As a consequence, whatever is written here has to be seen in this changed context. While all the basic and classic ideas presented here are equally applicable in the present circumstances, we need to modify the ways in which we apply them in the present context.

For example, work from home and online meetings have become the new norms in inter and intra office meetings involving white collar jobs. However, one can see a yearning as well as reluctance to get back to normalcy as soon as possible with abatement of the pandemic. Similarly, the phenomenal growth of online shopping has changed the ways in which products are promoted, stored, bought and delivered. These have given way to new business opportunities and have also led to the demise of many established ones. Integrated global supply chains are fraying at their ends to meet the supplies and demands from various parts of the world.

Driving all these is the relentless growth of the digital technologies. While this has brought in several advantages, it has also created many challenges. Navigating business in the digital world is the basic challenge faced by all companies and their managers.

With greater penetration of social media, people in all countries have become more aware of developments all over the world. As seen earlier, this has revolutionised the way people see and buy products and services. Brand loyalty based purely on premium image by multinational corporations (MNCs) is taking a beating with the emergence of "value for money" shift in consumer's minds. While more avenues for finance are available, pressures to control costs and offer robust profits to shareholders are proving to be great challenges in managing the finances of organisations.

Further, this has also brought in greater awareness among people on growing inequalities. It is an established fact that the rich, especially the very rich, have grown disproportionately rich and the poor, the bottom of the pyramid, have become poorer. Women empowerment as well as emerging groups like LGBT (lesbian, gay, bisexual and transgender) all need recognition and expect acceptance and opportunities available to others. Organisations cannot just stop at paying lip service to the concept of 'equal opportunity employer' but need to implement the same in letter and spirit.

In the current global political scenario, the so-called "superpowers" are flexing their muscles and are becoming more and more protective of their industries and territories. Emerging nations, having suffered suppression by them are also jostling for niche space more vigorously. A unipolar world that existed with the demise of Soviet Union is once again witnessing great rivalries between the two economic superpowers of USA and China. Both them and Russia are vying to be the leader in the global context with financial, trade and military might and unbridled ambition for expanding their territories and spheres of influence. These conflicts have created great tension and flareup among them and other nations which have aligned with them all over the world. At the same time, threat of nuclear warfare by any indiscriminate ruler in any one of these countries hangs heavily in the air and the United Nations has been reduced to a mute spectator. These have led to authoritarian leaders in many countries and democratic values and freedom of thought and expression have been curtailed.

How true this has played out is being seen by the unexpected invasion of Ukraine by Russia, started in February 2022. This war has been dragging on till today causing much human misery and disturbing the whole world with prospects of massive hunger caused by sudden breakdown of supply chains. The comity of nations is getting fractured, and the threat of nuclear warfare appears real. As far as business and management fields are concerned, companies have gone back to drawing boards to rewrite their supply chain configurations even as they have just started implementing new supply chain strategies as a fallout of Covid 19. Once again, inequalities are rising and while new millionaires are springing up fast, millions of people are staring at abject poverty.

With the devastating blow delivered by Covid 19, governments have once again become the major economic engines in most of these nations. Giant technological corporations that dominate the digital world are fighting fiercely to protect their turfs as well as make inroads into others' domains. In the process, they are dictating the ways we, the people, live since our modern lives depend on them. Governments are finding it more and more difficult to rein them in due to their financial and market powers.

Most of the world is facing the reality of environmental degradation and the growing green movement to protect the globe for the present and future generations is gathering force.

All these have naturally affected all organisations' priorities, objectives, strategies etc.

Summing up, we can say that "business as usual" or old ways of doing things will not work anymore. New, innovative ways need to be found to meet these challenges constantly in this ever-changing scenario. However, I would like to emphasise that these basic, classic concepts and ideas still hold good, and we need to modify the ways we practise them. The basic purpose of these booklets is to expose the readers to all these classic concepts that have stood the test of time in a simple and concise manner so that they can start thinking and working out how to put them in practice in the current context.

A.S. Srinivasan   **October, 2022**

A.S. Srinivasan

A.S. Srinivasan holds a bachelor's degree in Mechanical Engineering (from the University of Madras), a Post Graduate Diploma in Plastics Engineering (D.I.I.T. from the Indian Institute of Technology, Bombay) and a Master's degree in Business Management (M.B.M. from the Asian Institute of Management, Manila, Philippines). He has participated in the Global Program for Management Development of the University of Michigan Business School.

Srinivasan has over 25 years of experience in industry and 15 years of experience in academics and consulting. His industry experience is primarily in the areas of Marketing and General Management in companies like TI Cycles, Aurofood, Pierce Leslie and Cutfast.

His last assignment was with Chennai Business School, a start up business school in Chennai, for over two years. As the first Dean of the school, he developed and implemented the curriculum for the post graduate program in management for the first batch. Prior to that, he was working with Institute for Financial Management and Research (IFMR), Chennai, for 8 years looking after the partnership with the Open University Business School (OUBS), UK in offering their Executive MBA in India. Apart from handling courses in the PGDM program of IFMR, he was actively involved in offering Management Development Programs (MDPs) to corporates and in consultancy assignments.

His current interests are in the areas of Management, Business, Economics etc. where he would like to keep himself updated with recent developments. He has taken to publishing blogs on these subjects for private circulation.

A.S. Srinivasan
A1/3/4, "Srinivas", Third Main Road,
Besant Nagar, Chennai 600 090
Mobile: 91 98414 01721
Email: sansrini@gmail.com

Made in the USA
Monee, IL
08 July 2026